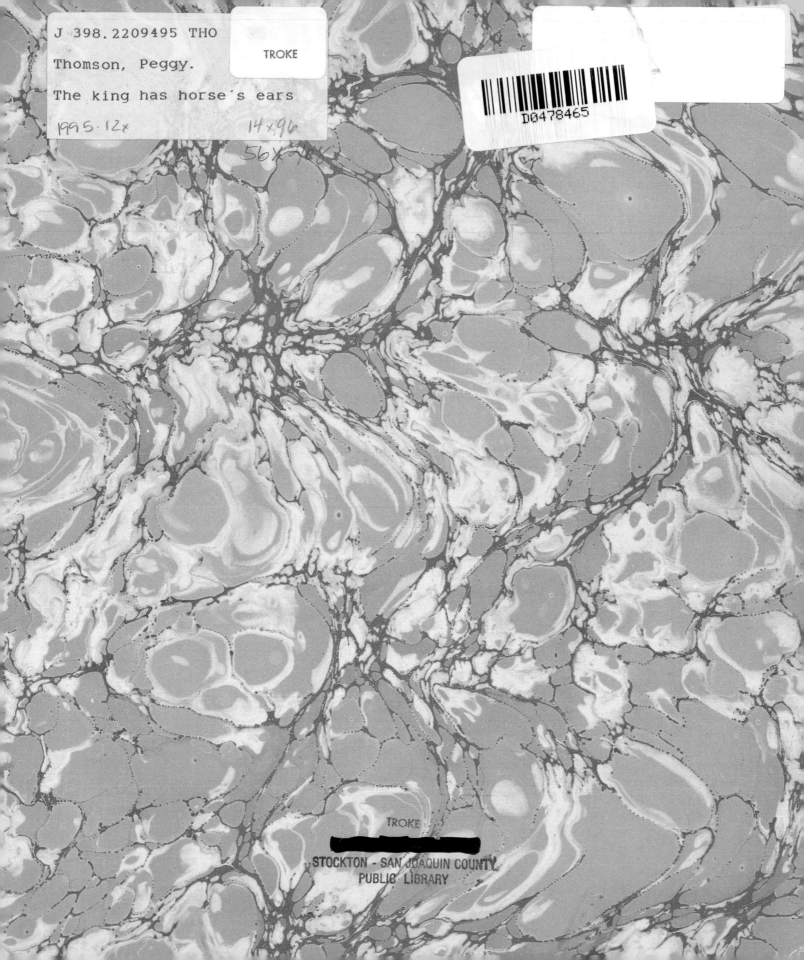

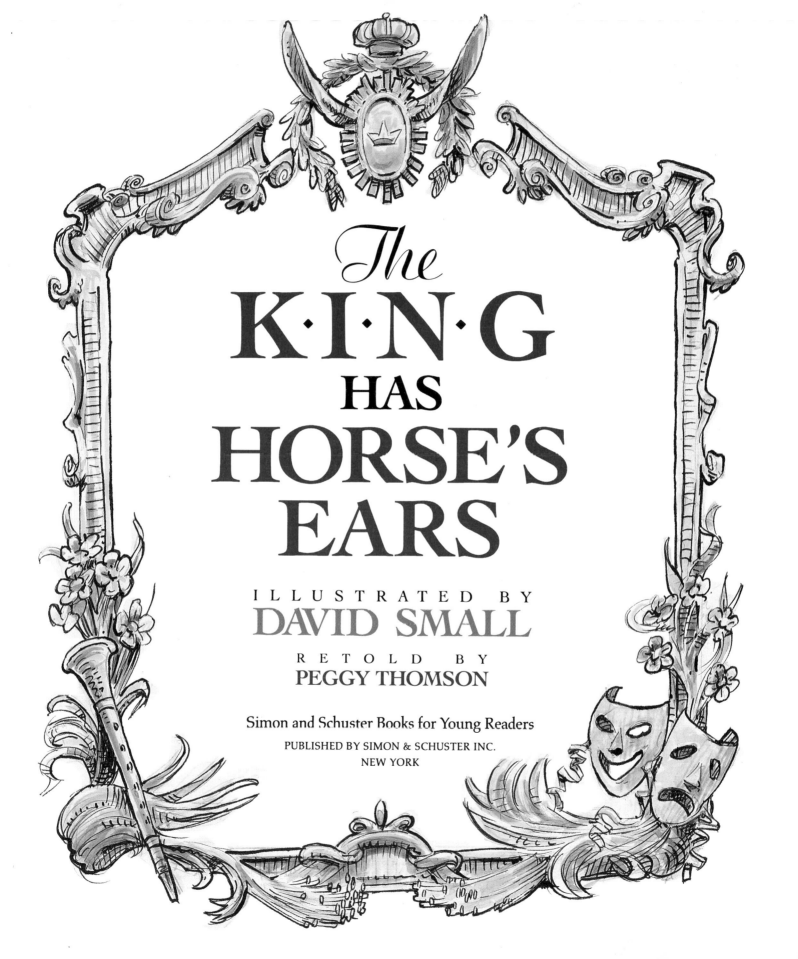

The
K·I·N·G
HAS
HORSE'S
EARS

ILLUSTRATED BY
DAVID SMALL

RETOLD BY
PEGGY THOMSON

Simon and Schuster Books for Young Readers

PUBLISHED BY SIMON & SCHUSTER INC.
NEW YORK

SIMON AND SCHUSTER
BOOKS FOR YOUNG READERS
Simon & Schuster Building
Rockefeller Center
1230 Avenue of the Americas
New York, New York 10020

10 9 8 7 6 5 4 3 2 1

J 398, 2209495 THO   FO
1497 288C
Library of Congress Cataloging-in-Publication Data
Thomson, Peggy.
The king has horse's ears, retold by Peggy Thomson:
illustrated by David Small.
p. cm.
SUMMARY: Only the king and his barber know that
the king has horse's ears, until the secret gets out
just in time for the king's wedding day.
1. Midas—Juvenile literature. [1. Midas. 2. Mythology,
Greek.] I. Small, David, 1945– ill. II. Title.
BL820.M55T48 1988
398.2'2'09495—dc19   87-35587
ISBN 0-671-64953-1   CIP
AC

For Sherry

D.S.

For my parents

P.T.

There once lived a king named Horace, who had everything a person could wish for: piles of gold and silver, a huge palace, closets full of clothes, a warm dog, and all the chocolate he could eat.

Everyone said, "What riches! What good fortune! How happy he must be!"

But Horace was not happy. In fact, he was miserable. For in addition to his wealth, his fine clothes, and his chocolate, Horace had a terrible secret.

Horace had horse's ears.

Most of the time, of course, they were hidden under his crown—and he was lucky to be king, for not everybody can wear a crown all the time without attracting attention. But poor Horace worried constantly that someone would find out about his ears.

The court barber was the only person who knew the king's secret because, after all, there are some things you can't do with a crown on, and getting your hair cut is one of them. The barber had been sworn to secrecy at pain of death, and every time the king went for a royal trimming, he reminded the barber of his oath: "If you ever tell a soul, I'll have you beheaded!"

The barber worried day and night that someone would discover the royal secret he carried. Soon the burden began to make him ill. He couldn't eat. He couldn't have fun. He couldn't sleep at night for fear that his lips would move during a dream. One day he looked in the mirror and, seeing how thin and pale he had become, he decided to pay a visit to the court doctor.

The doctor thumped him on the back, tapped him on the chest, and made him stick out his tongue and say "four-and-twenty blackbirds." Then he squinted at the barber and said "Hmmm" and "Ah-ha." Finally, he said, "You are in perfect health. I think it's your conscience that's bothering you. You have a terrible secret that is making you ill—I can see it all over your face."

The barber nearly fell on the floor. *It is just as I feared,* he thought. *It's written all over my face! Everyone on the street will be able to see it!*

"Now," continued the doctor, "my advice to you is that you tell me what it is, so ____"

"But I can't!" cried the barber, horrified. "I've been sworn to secrecy. I'll lose my head! Can't you just give me a pill instead?"

The doctor squinted some more, paced up and down, and said finally, "What if you let out your secret in a place where nobody can hear it?"

That seemed like a good idea. The barber left the doctor's office and wandered around the kingdom until he found a lonely spot by the water's edge. Bending down as close as he could without falling into the water, he whispered:

"The king has horse's ears! The king has horse's ears!"

Immediately he felt better. He breathed deeply, held his head up high, and heard the birds singing. What a relief! He hurried back to the palace, skipping a little on the way.

Several months later, the town was buzzing with news: the king was engaged to be married. Horace was preparing a huge celebration for thousands of people, ordering the fanciest foods, the choicest wines, and musicians from distant lands across the sea.

When the musicians arrived for the wedding, their boat passed by the very spot where the barber had revealed the king's secret.

A patch of reeds had sprung up from the ground, and one piper, remembering how old and worn his reed was, plucked a new one for the occasion.

After weeks of preparations, the wedding day arrived. The king and queen exchanged their vows, and there was much rejoicing. After a huge meal, Horace, handsome in his wedding robes, called for the musicians to play something to entertain the guests.

The piper stepped forward, took a deep breath, and put his pipe to his lips. But instead of the melody he had intended to play, out came:

THE KING
HAS
HORSE'S
EARS!

THE KING
HAS
HORSE'S
EARS!

Silence fell over the room. The guests looked at one another and started tittering. The piper shook his flute and stared at it. The king turned red in the face. The barber started looking for a place to hide.

"Off with your head!" cried the king, as he spotted the terrified barber cowering behind the ten-tier wedding cake. But he could barely make himself heard over the laughter of thousands of guests who were trying to catch a glimpse of his ears.

Just then the queen stepped forward. "Hush!" she com-
manded, and the room fell silent once again. Then she walked
over to Horace and tenderly removed the crown from his head.

"I think you have lovely ears," she said, touching them lightly. The king's ears twitched a little. "I wouldn't have you any other way."

After that, horse's ears became very popular. They were featured in the fashion column of the local newspaper,

1. Coiffure pour la Bourgeoise petite-maîtresse

2. Oreilles du Roi pendues

3. Bonnet à la Sultanne

4. Oreilles du Roi surmonté d'un pouf

desserts and streets
were named after them
and songs were written
about them.

Many people even started to wear
clip-on horse's ears in
all shapes, sizes, and colors,

and the barber did a
brisk business
grooming them.

As for the king, he never had to worry about hiding his ears again, and he and the queen lived a long and happy life in the castle.

Some secrets are better when they're shared.

THE END

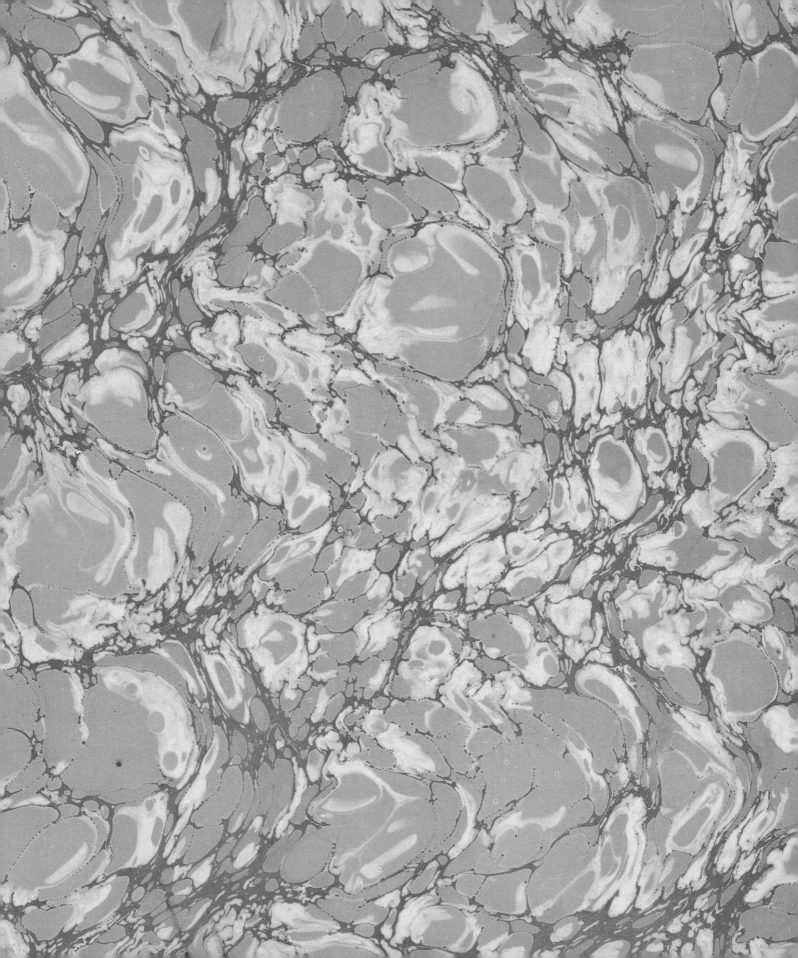